Landale's Cautionary Tales

Comic Verse for the 21ˢᵗ Century

James Landale

with

Illustrations by Mr. Tony McSweeney

CANONGATE

Edinburgh · New York · Melbourne

First published in Great Britain in 2006 by
Canongate Books Ltd, 14 High Street,
Edinburgh EH1 1TE

1

British Library Cataloguing-in-Publication Data
A catalogue record for this book is available on
request from the British Library

1 84195 847 6 (10-digit ISBN)
978 1 84195 847 7 (13-digit ISBN)

Typeset by Sharon McTeir, Creative Publishing Services
Printed and bound by GGP Media GmbH, Poessneck, Germany

www.canongate.net

For Ellen and Alexander

Contents

Introduction

Almost a century has passed since Hilaire Belloc first warned of the dreadful consequences of lying, eating bits of string and leaving nurses in a crowd. Over the years, successive generations of children have delighted in his verse, reciting the words with gusto, learning them by heart. In turn, these children have grown up and passed the tales on to their own sons and daughters. They have done so because there is an enduring brilliance to Belloc's work that allows it to survive the ages. Parents know it is just as wrong to lie now as it was in Belloc's day and so the deceitful Matilda must burn. Likewise, modern-day Sarah Byngs must learn to read so they can avoid furious bulls. And boys like John Vavassour De Quentin Jones must learn not to throw stones, even if the risk these days is not the loss of a fortune but the gain of an anti-social behaviour order.

And yet, in recent years, a small shadow of doubt has grown at the back of my mind. Is it just possible that perhaps, at last, some of Belloc's verse is beginning to show its age? Do today's children really think it the height of naughtiness to chew bits of string? Or slam doors? Or leave their nurse in a crowd? A colleague said he had trouble explaining to his children what a 'ball room floor' was and why Matilda's house might have one. Do children know what 'a bit of stiff' is, or who the Lord High Chamberlain may be, or why Charles Augustus Fortescue might wear cap, stockings and pinafore? Answer: probably not.

So it is timely, therefore, if a little presumptious, to offer some new cautionary tales to today's generation, a little poetic advice to address the sins of the 21st century. My aim is not to replace Belloc, but to extend him, bring him up to date and in the process, honour him. No one can ever match him.

The Ten Commandments may still be the best code of conduct devised to regulate man's behaviour. But we all need a few cautionary tales to fill in the gaps.

James Landale
August 2006

The tales

Percy

Who Swore and broke the Law

The foulest mouth I ever knew

Belonged to Percy Pelligrew,

A little boy who thought it fun

To swear and curse at everyone.

He'd say 'damn
this' and 'balls to
that'

And 'stuff it up
your effing hat',

'Buzz off', 'screw you', 'what utter crap!'

'Why don't you shut your ruddy trap?'

He simply could not speak without

Such vile invective pouring out;

Expletives Nixon deleted

He quite happily repeated.

He told his mum to naff off twice

Which wasn't really very nice.

His dad received a curt 'up yours'

For asking help with household chores.

And as for granny, Percy said

'She should by now be
bloody dead!'

The nanny too, though
very young

Had to endure his filthy
tongue

Till she, in exasperation

Left, as no remuneration

Is worth such
vituperation.

At last Percy came a cropper;

He swore at a Passing Copper

Who was distinctly unamused

To be so publicly abused

(No member of the Flying Squad

Likes to be called 'a Sodding Plod').

So he arrested Master P

For speaking such profanity

Because, as I have said before,

Swearing thus is against the law,

Under the Public Order Act,

Section Five – and that's a fact.

The parents of this boy of nine

Were forced therefore to pay a fine

And then bound over to ensure

That he would go and swear no more.

Moral:

Young boys may be, I've oft averred

Obscene only if never heard.

John

*Who was Unkind to Animals and
Paid the Consequence*

There never was a Boy so Cruel

As John de Granville Graham-Youll.

He could not pass a dog without

Giving the beast a Fearful Clout.

He liked to yank on Horses' Reins

And kick their Shins and pull their
Manes.

And as for cats, his Favourite Trick

Involved a Very Pointed Stick.

He tugged the Legs off
Spiders and

Whatever else would
come to hand.

With Limbless Slugs, his great resolve

Was watching them slowly dissolve

Beneath a Pinch of Salt, which he

Would sprinkle over liberally.

One day the lad – just
for a lark
Went off to a
Safari Park
In search of Creatures yet
to see
How cruel a teenage boy could be,
And there it was he came across
A Very Large Rhinoceros.

But though he Poked and Kicked at it,

The Rhino didn't care a bit.

For as we know, his Wrinkly Skin

Is very, very far from thin.

(As Mr Kipling described just so

In stories many years ago)

The Rhino, who was unaware

That Master John was even there

Decided it was Time to Sit

And crushed the boy a little bit.

And thus John keeps his *Derrière*

Forever in a Wheelchair.

The good news, I am glad to say

Is that John learned a lot that day

And now he fights to Save the Whale

But that is quite another tale.

Moral:

Unless you are that way inclined

Avoid approaching from behind.

Nicholas

*Who refused to Tidy his Bedroom
and Died Alone*

One thing that causes
much Distress

For parents is, of course,
the Mess

In which a child can
leave their room.

Oh how it makes them
Rage and Fume!

Now normally a child can be

Persuaded (eventually)

To rally to and Wave a Duster

So that their room can pass Muster.

But not so Nick, a Mogul's son

Who lived in Trendy Islington.

He never tidied up his room

And thus went early to his Doom.

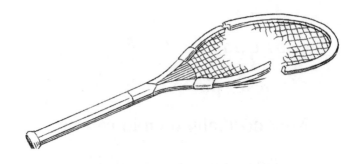

He left the place in such a state

It makes me shudder to
relate.

His Bed, of course, was never
made.

His clothes were everywhere
displayed.

Like so many north London boys

He never put away his toys:

Discarded Teddies, bits of Bike,

Boring jigsaws he didn't like,

Remote-control cars, Model Planes,

Double-O gauge electric trains,

Unread novels, an empty box,

A bag of useless Sandstone Rocks,

Computer games whose screens
were dim,

An Action Man with missing limb,

Cowboy guns, a festering sponge,

Batteries oozing Noxious Gunge.

There was within
this Habitat

Not room enough
to swing a cat!

Nick's parents tried
to get the lad

To tidy up his
Squalid Pad

But he had long
taken the view

That this work
was not his to do.

The room was such a mess that he

One day got lost and Missed his Tea.

Not only that, his Supper too

Which for a boy will never do.

His parents called the Police and more

Who struggled through the bedroom door

But even they got stuck amid

The mess and never found the kid.

So some days later it transpired

That the Slovenly Boy expired

Of Starvation, and not before

He'd wished he'd tidied up some more.

Moral:

Do not get lost in north London

Without a decent packed luncheon.

Gregory

*Who Listened but Did Not Hear
and was Silenced Forever*

Gregory was a Silly Sod

Who never turned off
his iPod.

All day and night his
headphones hissed

As he ran through his long
playlist

Of all those Ghastly Modern
Bands

That no parent
understands.

In consequence
of this, therefore,

He never heard,
one day, the roar

Of an approaching
Wild Boar

Which knocked him
off his feet, it's true,

But cut down on
his listening too.

For now Greg spends
more time with God

Who confiscated his iPod

And said that Silence would instead

Be better for a boy who's Dead.

Moral:

If you wish to reach old age

Download silence from Mr Cage.

Evangeline

Who paid the Ultimate Price for television

Evangeline Smyth, known as Evie,

Died young from watching Too Much TV.

A slothful girl from Enfield Locks

She spent all day before the box.

Her eyes to the screen were glued;

She rarely paused Except for Food.

All day long – there she sat.

No wonder she became So Fat.

She slouched so long inside her chair

That soon not just her eyes were square.

And it was all that she could do

To get up to go to the loo.

One day in spring it happened that

The food ran out inside her flat.

For most of us, it's no big deal

To miss out on the evening meal.

But for Ms Smyth, the Shock was Great

She flew into a Grievous State

And rang for Pizza, Fish and Chips

And Curries Hot that scald your lips.

But everywhere she was told

'Your call is valued: can you hold?'

So thus famished, with Rumbling Tum

Ms Smyth got off her Bulging Bum

And left the flat to Forage Wide

For food enough for her inside.

But as she crossed the road, her gaze

Was captured by the vast arrays

Of TVs in the TV shop.

Thus mesmerised, she had to stop.

Her Favourite Soap! A Crucial Plot!

But in her daze she failed to spot

The Fast Approaching
Omnibus

Which knocked her flat
and squashed her thus:

And so she joined that
home so high

For Couch Potatoes in
the Sky.

Moral:

The moral is, I have to say,

Always send for takeaway.

Amelia

*Who Chewed Gum and
Lost her Shoes*

Amelia Florence Erskine-Crum

Was Very Fond of Chewing Gum.

Day in, day out, her dainty jaw

Would grind in revolutions for

As a Gangster's Teenage Wife

She led a rather Stressful Life

And found that if she chewed all day

She kept the Stress and Strains at bay.

Not only that it also cured

The Halitosis she'd endured

Ever since her father's death:

She had inherited his Breath

As well as all the Cash that won

The darling heart of her felon.

Now Melly had a Nasty Trait:

Like many folk who masticate,

She thought it Very Right and Meet

To spit her gum out in the street!

Oh, was ever there in our youth

A trend so Ghastly and Uncouth?

It's not that she was unaware

That leaving gum bits everywhere

Is wrong – it's just she didn't care.

Until one day she Pushed her Luck,

Trod in some herself, and Was Stuck.

So sticky was this gummy ball

She couldn't move her feet at all.

But did this worry Mrs Crum?

Why, no Sir, not at all, By Gum!

She simply abandoned her shoes

(Even though they were Jimmy Choos!)

And hurried home in Bare Feet

So that she could fulfil and meet

The curfew that her ASBO had

Laid down for being Drunk and Bad.

The strictures of her magistrate

Being that she never could be late.

And so today young Mrs Crum

Always makes sure she Wraps her Gum.

Though married to an Awful Thug

She is at least No Litterbug.

Moral:

It's not only Presidents who

Must synchronise their walk and chew.

Anthony

Who Found Relief in Death Alone

For Anthony, there were No Doubts;

    Small boys like him should not
    eat Sprouts

        Or Beans or Greens of
        any sort.

        His bowels became
        thus Somewhat
        Taut,

    Deprived as they were of
    cabbage

And all other kinds of Roughage.

Now most of us do what we can

With some Dried Fruit and Bowls of
Bran.

But this Colonic Formula

For keeping people regular

Was unknown to the little lad

Whose insides went from Good to Bad

Whereby he swelled up, just like this –

Until he burst in deathly bliss.

Thus he died, his life Truncated

Just from Being Constipated.

Moral:

If you can't go when others can

Do not be stubborn – Eat Your Bran!

Harry

Who Took Drugs and Perished Miserably

The Chief Defect of Harry
Hope

Was that he used Far Too
Much Dope.

Not only this, but
other things

Such as the Kind Drug
Dealer brings,

Like Crack and Smack
and LSD

And Naughty
Cookies for his tea.

He Chased the Dragon,
he sniffed glue,

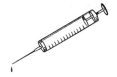

There's nothing that he
didn't do.

Steroids, Valium,
ecstasy

He was a Human
Pharmacy!

Now Harry was, of course, a
Fool

Who thought that
taking drugs was Cool.

He knew the stuff was
Dangerous

But he just thought:
'How Glamorous!'

And so he lost the chance to
mend

His ways before he
met his end.

For once he took so much that he

Became inside Incendiary.

His breath was ready to ignite!

So when he lit a Marlboro Light

He blew himself to Kingdom Come

Which all his friends thought Rather
Dumb.

His parents, who were not
impressed

Bade all the children
round attest:

Regardless how you get your
thrills,

Always remember
– Smoking Kills.

Norman

Who became Rich despite his Title

Many teenagers
wish they had

               The right to choose
               their Mum and Dad

And this was
certainly the wish

               Of Norman Vere,
               Lord Cavendish.

His folks, despite their Noble Name

Were for him a Source of Shame

For often they embarrassed Norm

With gauche displays of rank bad form:

His dad would pinch his Girlfriends' Bums,

His mother Chatted Up his Chums.

They kissed him outside
the school gate

(Which, as we know,
all children hate),

And worst of all,
they'd both insist

On dancing what they
called 'the Twist'

At parties where
they'd tap their feet

And say: 'This one's
got a Good Beat.'

Not only this, they'd
Drink and Smoke

And snort, from time
to time, some coke

And talk enormous
tosh till late

Without a thought
for what they ate:

Chocolate, chips
and takeaway,

Whereby their bums
grew day by day.

For all Norm's parents' lineage,

They were Distinctly Average

Members of our Ancient Peerage.

Not so Norman, not so Lord C;

He behaved Quite Differently.

He washed his face, he never lied

He always was Most Dignified.

Unlike most Veres, he was no fool

And actually attended school

Where he thrived on Verbs and Sums

And learned to play the Kettledrums

And filled his brain with Useful Fact.

He ate three meals and Never Snacked;

Incredibly he liked his greens,

His favourite being large Broad Beans!

But most of all he adored sport;

He was a very active sort.

Eventually his example

Led his Aged Ps to sample

The Healthy Life. They stopped
the booze

And fags and bought some
Running Shoes

Whereby they both had Heart Attacks

And fell down dead upon their Backs.

Thus Norm achieved the Viscountcy

And by some neat Accountancy

Also became rather wealthy,

Which goes well with being healthy

Sadly, though, Norman spent the lot

On a large, vulgar Motor Yacht,

A New Bathroom with Gold Taps

And several nasty Burberry Caps,

And worst of all, an oh-so-nice

White Rolls-Royce with furry dice.

NOBLESSE OBLING

Moral:

Do not expect Gentility

In all of the Nobility.

Jonathan

Who Picked More than his Nose

Young Jonathan
would often stick

His finger up
his Nose and pick

Whatever he could
find up there.

One day he probed
Without Due Care

And went so
far he Picked
his Brain!

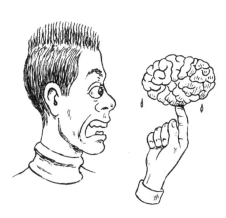

He never was the same
again.

Moral:

Oroficial exploration
Is but good in moderation.

Rose

*Who drank Too Much and was once the
Worse for Underwear*

If you saw Rose
you'd never think

She ever took a
Single Drink.

She looked so sweet,
so pure, so prime

And this she was
– most of the time.

But come weekends, she was Unhinged;

She went out on the tiles and Binged

On Vodka Red Bull, rum and coke,

Tequila shots that made her choke,

Alcopops, and gin and tonic,

In short All That's Alcoholic

(Quite unlike her sister Mandy

Who preferred a glass of shandy).

Now when Rose got drunk, she behaved

In ways that were, well, Quite
Depraved.

She'd shout abuse
and get in fights,

She'd let the boys
into her tights,

She'd stagger in the
streets and hurl

Her guts up. What
a Ghastly Girl!

One night, alas,
she went too far

And Showed her
Chest off to a bar

And thus was
subject to arrest

In punishment for
Baring Breast.

But worst of all,
the police, you see

Were shadowed
by a BBC

Camera crew,
who filmed the lot!

And so, of course,
each dreadful shot

Now gets repeated
on the news

When they report
on Youth and Booze.

And though they cover up her eyes,

For some things there is No Disguise.

Her father, who was furious

And naturally abstemious

Confined poor Rose within her room

Until once more she was in Bloom

And ready never more to binge

In ways that made her parents cringe.

Moral:

Unless you have a Handsome Chest

It's always better to be dressed.

James

Who Played and Lost

There was a boy whose name
was James.

He loved to play computer games.

All day long he'd tap and scroll

And wiggle things on his console.

Lord! What a busy life he had!

Such battles between
Good and Bad!

He'd shoot and
bomb and go on
quests,

He'd slay dragons
and other pests,

He'd blast away at
villains and

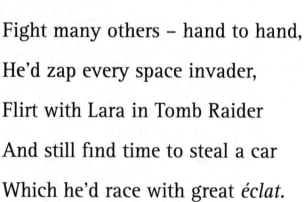

Fight many others – hand to hand,

He'd zap every space invader,

Flirt with Lara in Tomb Raider

And still find time to steal a car

Which he'd race with great *éclat*.

But too much of a good thing can

Be bad for you – as this young man

Found out one day when he confused

Real life with all these games he used.

In short, they drove him round the

bend

And thus James met a dreadful end:

As he left the house one morning

Some elves appeared without warning

And as they chased him down the road

He switched his coat into 'stealth mode'

And fired off a lethal volley

From his new pump-action brolly

But this jammed, so he was required

To steal a car from which he fired

An anti-elf neutron device

(It's done by sounding the horn twice)

But sadly his luck did not last:

As he escaped, driving fast,

James crashed the car! It fell apart!

Game over – time to press restart.

But none of this, of course, was real

Except, alas, the steering wheel

Against which lay poor James' head;

Bloody, staring and very dead.

Moral:

Do not play games all day in bed;

It can do odd things to your head.

Gloria

*Who made the Wrong Call
and was rendered Permanently
Incommunicado*

Gloria Bone was Apt to
Drone

All day upon her Mobile
Phone.

The moment she got out of
bed

She clamped the thing fast to
her head

And would put it down only if

Her signal was a tad Skew-Whiff.

She called her friends, she called her mates

She talked dirty to Billy Bates

She took photos, she played games

She texted boys with Funny Names.

And as for ringtones, everyday

They changed but never in a way

That made them sound any better.

She never wrote a Single Letter

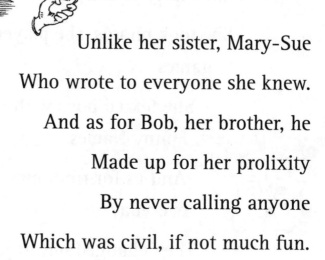

Unlike her sister, Mary-Sue

Who wrote to everyone she knew.

And as for Bob, her brother, he

Made up for her prolixity

By never calling anyone

Which was civil, if not much fun.

Now Gloria's mum, Mrs Bone

Naturally would not condone

Her girl's addiction to the phone

But was convinced (by her) that she

Required it for Security,

A premise that was False because

Her lambkin's phone line always was

Engaged – so mum could not get through

However much she wanted to.

One day Miss B was in the street

Not looking where she put her feet

(As ever, on her telephone)

She missed an Orange Warning
Cone

And plummeted into a hole

Whereby she joined the
Lord's Payroll

And was shocked to learn
that heaven

Has worse coverage than
Devon.

Moral:

When buying phones, it's no faux pas

To get one with a good radar.

Lord Faversham

Who Kissed and Lost

Lord Faversham, like many earls

Was very keen on kissing girls.

He could not pass a young lass by

Without trying to catch her eye

And if one stopped and said 'hullo'

He'd dive on in like Billy-Ho

And stick his tongue Straight Down
her Throat

(Which is Bad Form – all boys, please
note).

The peer just simply
loved to snog;

In short, he was a
randy dog

Who had
much more
testosterone

Than is good
for one
boy
alone.

He kissed
Susanna
from
next
door

And her
French
au pair,
Marie-Laure

And Geraldine,
the nanny who

Did *everything* he wanted to.

The Whitfeld twins did not resist

His charms and took turns to be kissed

While Vicki, Lady Balderdash,

Was all over him like a rash.

Sadly such promiscuity

Can't last in perpetuity

And Lord F found one day that he

Had got some ghastly STD

That meant, alas, his tongue fell off!

So now this Noble, Horny Toff,

Thus limited in his physique,

Can only peck girls on the cheek.

Moral:

If you are sex starved and young

It's good at times to hold your tongue.

Jennifer

Who Never Learned to Count and thus her days were Numbered

Jennifer was the sort of kid

Who muddled through in all she did.

Her aim in life was to get by

Without ever having to try

Too hard – and though she was no fool,

It meant she did not thrive at school.

The girl just didn't give a toss;

A time-honoured teenage ethos!

Jenny could read a bit, it's true

But never an entire book through.

She also spoke *un petit peu*

Of French, which was enough for her.

While geography made her head ache

She grasped at least the ox-bow lake

And though science was tough to learn

She made in time her Bunsen burn.

But as for numbers, no amount

Of teaching taught her how to count.

Now much to the disgust of Jen

Her brother, Nick, could count to ten

And even Ann – the baby – knew

That four was made from two plus two.

But no, the girl could not make sense

Of numbers and the consequence

Was grave indeed as you shall hear.

For once, when in her thirteenth year

Jenny was home and all alone

When fire struck but at the phone

She scanned the buttons in distress

Not knowing which she had to press.

She wanted to dial 999

But got instead upon the line

(From pressing buttons anyhow)

The butcher and a man from Slough.

Yet not once could she call the aid

Of the much needed fire brigade

And so the poor innumerate

Went breathless, burning to her fate.

Moral:

A little learning is dangerous

But even less is even worse.

Julia

Who Shopped until she was Dropped

Julia Smithson got her Kicks

From shopping hard at Harvey Nicks

And other emporia where

She bought more clothes than she
could wear;

A frock, once placed Against Her Chest,

Would almost always be purchased.

For Julia had
Great Passion

For what magazines
call Fashion;

She just never
learned to ration

Her appetites –
and, oh my dear,

It cost her, as you
now shall hear.

Her father, a millionaire,

Naturally became aware

Just how much his Darling
Heir

Was spending on her Underwear.

Thus impoverished, he at once

Forbad her her inheritance.

So now she is an ex-
heiress

Who works weekends at
M&S.

Moral:

If you Shop until you Drop
One day the Trust Fund will Stop.

Edward

Who got more of a Lie-in than he bargained for

Edward Villiers, known as Ted,

Was very slow to go to bed.

His *au pair* (French and not much use)

Accepted nightly his excuse

Of having urgently to read

A few more stories or his need

To spend a little Time and Care

Choosing that night's Teddy Bear.

He'd also want a drink, a Pee

Another bounce upon her Knee.

In short, anything to delay

The moment when he Hit the Hay.

Now Ted was not
especially bad:

He just longed
for his mum and dad

Who stayed out
late at Work and Gym

Instead of spending
time with him,

Neglect that in time
Sealed his Fate.

For one night, when he stayed up late

He fell asleep but was so tired

He never woke and thus expired.

Moral:

Don't wait for parents. Go to bed.

Wake them up at night instead!

Freddie

*Whose Curiosity got the
better of him*

Freddie Fitz,
the Viscount
Farquhar

Was a dreadful
nosy parker.

A curious boy,
he loved to pry

Where he should
not – in short, to
spy.

He would eavesdrop
conversations,

Snoop on private
assignations

But most of all
he liked to shock

By opening doors
without a knock:

He heard his sister
talking dirty;

His aunt claiming
she was thirty.

He saw his
brother kick a dog,

His teacher have
a naughty snog.

In everything
he poked his nose

To see just what
he could expose.

Until one ill-fated
morning –

He went upstairs
without warning

And caught his parents in the nude

Engaged in something rather rude,

A sight that left him open-eyed

And shamed for having ever pried.

He thus learned that a peer – it's true

Is what you are, not what you do.

Moral:

All Peeping Toms! You should know this:

That sometimes Ignorance is Bliss.